This Book belongs to
..................,
who knows when to
STAND UP and
SPEAK UP!

FOR WILLIAM AND CHARLOTTE

All rights reserved. Published in the United States by Schwartz & Wade Books,
an imprint of Random House Children's Books, a division of Penguin Random House LLC, New York.

Schwartz & Wade Books and the colophon are trademarks of Penguin Random House LLC.

Visit us on the Web! rhcbooks.com
Educators and librarians, for a variety of teaching tools, visit us at RHTeachersLibrarians.com

Library of Congress Cataloging-in-Publication Data is available upon request.
ISBN 978-0-593-30158-6 (hc) — ISBN 978-0-593-30159-3 (lib. bdg.) — ISBN 978-0-593-30160-9 (ebook)

The text of this book is set in 34-point Whitman Bold.
The illustrations were rendered digitally in the Procreate app.

MANUFACTURED IN CHINA
1 3 5 7 9 10 8 6 4 2

STAND UP! SPEAK UP!

A story inspired by the Climate Change Revolution

by Andrew Joyner

schwartz & wade books · new york

Wake up.

Dress up.

Drink up.

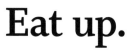

Eat up.

Meet up.

Signs up.

Cheer up.

Finish up.

Eat up.

Drink up.

Stay up.

Rest up.

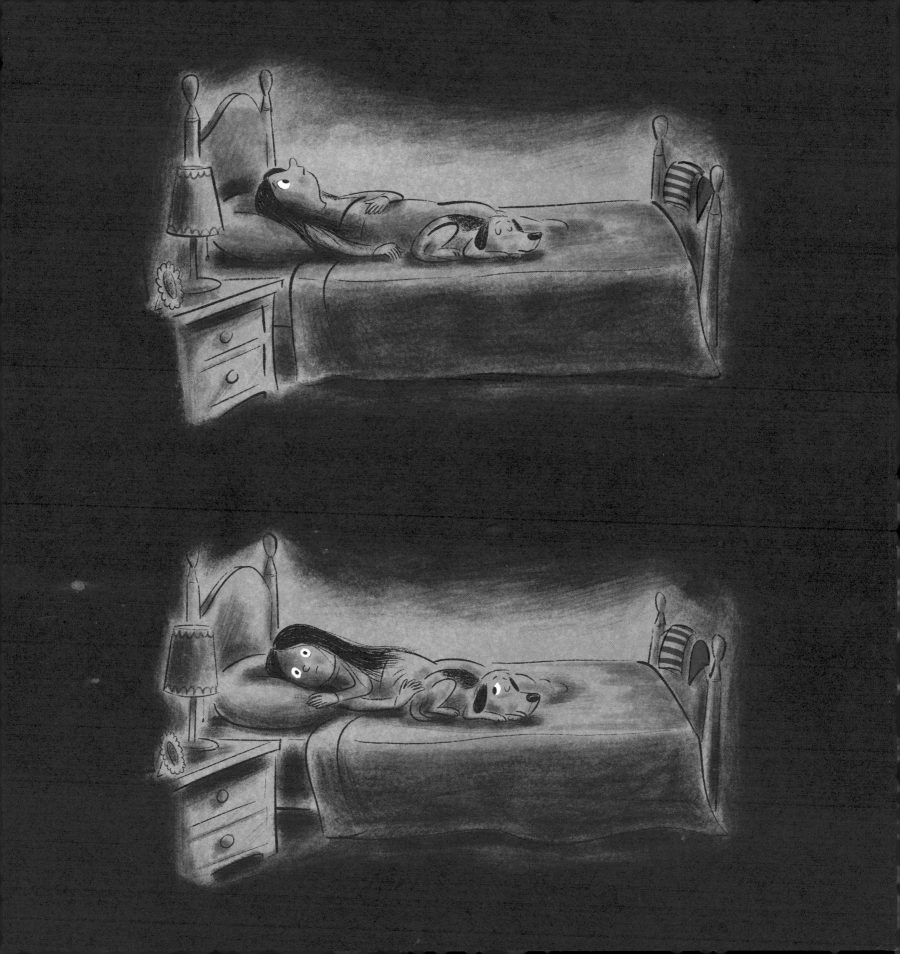

Still up.

Think up.

Write up.

Listen up.

Turn up.

Stand up. Speak up.

Hands up.

Sign up.

Young people everywhere are STANDING UP and SPEAKING UP!

AUTUMN PELTIER

Autumn Peltier is a water warrior from the Wiikwemkoong First Nation. She is inspired to protect water by her ancestor Great Auntie Bidaasige-ba. In 2019, when Autumn was fifteen years old, she spoke at the United Nations General Assembly. "One day I will be an ancestor," she said, "and I want my descendants to know I used my voice so they can have a future."

MARINEL UBALDO

Marinel Ubaldo survived typhoon Haiyan, which killed more than six thousand people when it struck the Philippines in 2013. Marinel petitioned the Philippines Commission on Human Rights to get fossil fuel companies to take responsibility for the damage caused by climate change.

HILDA FLAVIA NAKABUYE

Hilda Flavia Nakabuye of Uganda spends every weekend cleaning up plastic and tells the world what it's like to live with climate change in Africa. In 2019 she visited Denmark to speak to leaders from around the world. "Rest assured," she said, "that youth from the other side of the world are fighting for a safe future for you and for us all and are not about to give up."

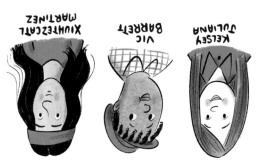

KELSEY JULIANA **VIC BARRETT** **XIUHTEZCATL MARTINEZ**

In 2015, Kelsey Juliana, Vic Barrett, Xiuhtezcatl Martinez, and eighteen other young people stood up to the United States government. They took the government to court! The court case is called Juliana v. United States, but to the twenty-one young plaintiffs, it is known as Youth v. Gov. They want the courts to order the government to protect their constitutional right to a clean and safe planet.

Jamie Margolin and Nadia Nazar met online and started the youth climate movement called Zero Hour. Jamie works with climate activists around the world. Nadia uses her art to get people thinking about climate change.

In 2016, Mari Copeny wrote a letter to the president. She wanted President Barack Obama's help cleaning the polluted water in her hometown of Flint, Michigan. President Obama read the letter and decided to visit Mari in Flint. After meeting her, he gave money and resources to help make Flint's water safe.

Isra Hirsi founded the US Youth Climate Strike and has helped organize many climate change protests throughout the United States.

Every week, Alexandria Villaseñor demonstrates outside the United Nations building in New York, asking world leaders to take serious action on climate change.

Elsa Mengistu is a climate activist and organizer at Zero Hour. She works to make her college campus more environmentally friendly.

Xiye Bastida Patrick is a member of the Otomi-Toltec Nation and an organizer of Fridays for Future in New York. The Otomi-Toltec Nation believes that if we care for the earth, then it will care for us. So Xiye has been talking to governments, committees, corporations, and other young people about the climate crisis, all while also finishing high school.

On August 20, 2018, Greta Thunberg skipped school to sit outside Sweden's Parliament House, holding a sign that said "Skolstrejk för klimatet," or "School strike for climate." Her protest has inspired young people all over the world to take action on climate change. To talk and lobby and march and rally and think and write and create. To stand up and speak up!